"Hey!" Wishbone saw someone's leg disappear into the dark maze ahead.

Wishbone barked. "Let's follow him—or her. Maybe we'll get out of here."

But Joe pulled his leash in the other direction. Wishbone wouldn't budge.

"Come on, Wishbone," Joe called.

Wishbone held his ground. "I don't think we should."

He changed his mind when he saw wire bins filled with a lot of balls. Wishbone went through a doorway with Joe and Sam.

Then the door slammed shut be-hind them.

"What's going on?" Sam asked.

Wishbone lis-tened. Something heavy was being  shoved against the door. "Some*one* or some*thing* is blocking us in!"

Books in the
wishbone™
The Early Years series:

Jack and the Beanstalk

The Sorcerer's Apprentice

Hansel and Gretel

*The Brave Little Tailor**

*coming soon

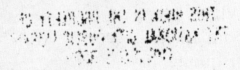

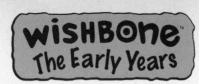

WISHBONE™
The Early Years

Hansel and Gretel

by Vivian Sathre
WISHBONE™ created by Rick Duffield

Little Red Chair Books

Little Red Chair Books™, *A Division of **Lyrick Publishing**™*

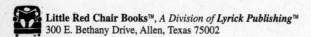 **Little Red Chair Books**™, *A Division of Lyrick Publishing*™
300 E. Bethany Drive, Allen, Texas 75002

©1999 Big Feats Entertainment, L.P.

Edited by Pam Pollack

Copy edited by Jonathon Brodman

Continuity editing by Grace Gantt

Cover design by Lyle Miller

Cover painting and interior illustrations by Kathryn Yingling

Library of Congress Catalog Number: 99-61259

ISBN: 1-57064-741-0

First Printing: November 1999

10 9 8 7 6 5 4 3 2 1

Printed in the United States of America

For the students, teachers, parents,
and librarians who have welcomed
me into their hearts and schools

A WORD FROM OUR TOP DOG . . .

Helllooo! Wishbone here. Welcome to my brand-new series of books, Wishbone: The Early Years. These books tell the story of my adventures as a puppy, when my best friend, Joe, and his friends were eight years old and in the third grade.

In this story my friends and I go to a school carnival. We get tricked and end up trapped in a closet. This reminds me of the classic tale **"Hansel and Gretel."** I imagine that I am a young boy named Hansel. My sister, Gretel, and I fall into real danger when we meet a sharp-toothed, fishy-smelling, beady-red-eyed witch.

You're in for a real treat, so pull up a chair, grab a snack, and sink your teeth into *Hansel and Gretel!*

Chapter One

Carnival Time!

Wishbone nibbled from his food dish in the kitchen. Eating was one of the puppy's favorite pastimes! His best friend, Joe Talbot, and Joe's mom, Ellen, were there, too. Joe and Ellen were his people. And he was their Jack Russell terrier. Both of his people had dark hair. Wishbone's own coat was short and white. He also had great-looking brown and black spots.

Joe and Ellen were getting ready to go to a school carnival. Joe had been talking excitedly about it all week.

"I can't wait till we get there." Joe gave Wishbone a bowlful of fresh water. "We are going to have so much fun. This school carnival is

1

going to be the best one Oakdale Elementary has ever had!"

Ellen smiled.

"So what are we waiting for?" Wishbone trotted to Joe's side. He wagged his tail back and forth. "Uh . . . what's a school carnival?"

Suddenly, Wishbone raised his ears high. *Footsteps—on the front porch!*

"Company!" the puppy called. He heard knocking and ran to the door.

Joe and Ellen followed him.

"Is it Sam? Is it? Is it?" Wishbone danced around in a circle until Joe opened the door. There stood a smiling blond girl about Joe's height. "It is! Hi, Sam!" Wishbone sprang into the air. "Let me give your face a big lick! Oops—missed." Wishbone jumped higher. "Missed again. I'll get it right this time. . . ." Wishbone sprang even higher.

"Down, boy," Joe said.

Samantha Kepler—"Sam" for short—was one of Joe's best friends. Wishbone's, too. Sam was eight years old and a third-grader at Oakdale Elementary School, just like Joe. She enjoyed playing ball. *And* she always had time to give Wishbone a good scratch!

"Sam! Sam! Sam!" Wishbone barked until Sam leaned down and scratched him behind his ears. "Oh, that feels so good! You people should try it sometime."

"Hi, Mrs. Talbot. Hi, Joe," Sam said.

"Hi," Joe and Ellen replied together.

Sam waved at the car parked at the curb. "My dad said to thank you for taking me to the carnival."

Ellen nodded. "I invited Wanda to come, too. She'll be here any minute. Come on in and wait."

Wanda Gilmore lived next door to the Talbots. She always had really great flowers growing in her yard. They were surrounded by lots of good digging dirt. But she didn't like sharing the dirt with Wishbone.

"Joe, go next door and tell David we're ready to go," Ellen said.

Wishbone snapped his head around and faced the door. "Bigger footsteps!" he said.

"Knock-knock. Yoo-hoo!" Wanda called out. She let herself in, then closed the door. "Is it time to go?" A wide, flat hat sat on her head. It reminded Wishbone of a pizza.

"Soon, Wanda," Ellen said. She turned to Joe. "Put Wishbone on the leash before you go for David."

"Oooh!" Wishbone danced around while Joe went to get the leash.

Then Joe tried to hook it onto Wishbone's collar. "Hold still, boy."

"I don't know if I like the leash or not."

Wishbone licked Joe's face. Joe clipped the leash onto his collar. "It gets me outside, but I can't run around by myself. You follow me everywhere!"

Joe left to get David. He returned a few minutes later.

"David's right behind me," Joe told his mom. "Come on, Sam. We'll wait in the car."

Wishbone wagged his tail. David trotted across the sidewalk that connected his house and Joe's.

"Ready?" Joe asked, as David walked up.

"Yep." David smiled.

David Barnes was Joe and Wishbone's other best friend. David was one smart third-grader. He could figure out and build anything. He also always had time for a game of fetch. And unlike *some* people, David *liked* to have Wishbone play in his yard.

"Okay, let's go!" Wishbone led Joe and the kids out to Ellen's car. When Joe opened one of the side doors, Wishbone hopped in first. "Window seat! Thank you!"

Joe climbed in next, then David and Sam.

"Hi," David said, greeting Ellen and Wanda as they came out to the car.

Wanda looked at him and smiled. "Well, hi, there, David."

"Oakdale Elementary, here we come," Ellen said, as everyone put their seat belts on. Then she backed out of the driveway. "Do all of you have your carnival tickets?"

"Yes," the kids answered together.

"Ellen, you must have mine," Wishbone said.

Wanda looked over her shoulder and smiled at the kids. She owned the town newspaper, *The Oakdale Chronicle*. She had helped prepare for the carnival by placing free ads in the paper for a week. "I hear this is going to be a wonderful carnival."

Joe grinned. "They're having all the regular stuff, like a cake walk and a fishing booth."

Wishbone looked at Joe. "Fishing? Uh . . . cats aren't invited, are they?"

Joe continued. "Plus, they're having this game in the gym called The Mad Maze. It's for kids only."

"What is a Mad Maze?" Wishbone asked.

Wanda leaned around farther in her seat. "Tell me more!"

"Hello, anyone?" Wishbone tried again.

David leaned forward. "It's *so* scary that you have to be at least a third-grader to play."

"Oh." Wishbone stood on Joe's lap and stared into his face. "I'm not even a year old, Joe. Maybe if I stand real tall, they'll think I'm older."

"Oh!" Wanda said. "The Mad Maze sounds like a lot of fun."

"We'll let you know," Joe said.

Wishbone looked at the kids. "Helllooo! Puppy speaking." He stretched his neck as much as he could. And he tried to point his ears straight up. "How old do I look now?"

"The maze game is going to be fun," Sam said. "You can choose two or three different paths. Only one path takes you to the end. *And* every time you make it through the maze, you get a coupon from a box called the treasure box. The coupon has the name of your prize printed on it." Sam smiled. "The neat thing is that there's one *big* prize—a Space Jumpers game."

Wishbone sighed. "I can't wait till I'm fully grown. Then they'll listen to me."

"I've heard of that," Wanda said. "It's some kind of computer game."

Ellen drove up to the school and parked.

"It's a brand-new, hand-held computer game." Joe unbuckled his seat belt. He held Wishbone in his arms. "It's *so* cool. The game *talks* to the player."

"Yeah." David's face lit up. "The kids in the game have been sent away from Earth by bad guys. They're lost in space!"

"It's the player's job to get them home again," Joe added.

"Maybe one of us will win the big prize." Sam opened her door when Joe opened the one on his side.

"That would be awesome." Joe jumped out of the car with the puppy in his arms.

Wishbone squirmed. "The ground, Joe—I want to go down."

Finally, Joe set the puppy on the grass.

Wishbone sniffed the air. "I can smell popcorn! And it's close by."

"Joe, before you three kids go, let me review the ground rules with you," Ellen said. "Be careful. Keep an eye on Wishbone. And meet me and Wanda back at the car in two hours. Okay?"

The three kids nodded, and the puppy wagged his tail.

"We'll see you later, Mom," Joe said. Joe, Sam, and David followed Wishbone.

"Have fun." Ellen pointed toward the crowd by the flagpole. "Wanda and I are going to watch the jugglers."

Joe waved.

"What should we try first?" Sam looked around.

"How about all the snacks?" Wishbone suggested.

Joe glanced at the large crowd by the flagpole. He smiled. "I bet *everyone* will be watching the jugglers." He looked to Sam and David.

"Are you thinking what I'm thinking?" Sam asked.

9

Wishbone took a step toward her. "Does it have to do with food?"

David raised his eyebrows. "That nobody will be in line to play The Mad Maze game?"

"Yep!" Sam said, as she, Joe, and David raced toward the gym.

Wishbone ran between Joe and Sam. Sam's blond ponytail swayed from side to side. "Slow down, Joe!" Wishbone said. "You're passing up some really good ground smells. And I just stepped on something sticky! Let's check it out." But Joe didn't slow down.

They rounded a corner just outside the gym. Only two girls stood in line for The Mad Maze game. A big boy sat by the door to take tickets.

Running toward them from the other side of the building was Damont Jones. Damont was another classmate of Joe's. Both of the boys played basketball. Both played pretty good. Damont also liked to play tricks on people.

"I think there's trouble ahead!" Wishbone barked.

When Damont saw the group, he ran

faster. He leaped. Damont landed in line the same time as Joe, Sam, and David.

"Hey, Joe." Damont nudged Joe out of his way. "You have to be quick to beat me."

"I'm here to try to win the big prize in The Mad Maze game," Joe told the boy. "Not beat you in a race."

"You tell him, Joe!" Wishbone said, as he chewed on Joe's shoelace.

Damont glanced at Sam and David. "None of you has a chance with me here."

"We'll see." Sam smiled.

A minute later the boy taking tickets opened the door. The two girls at the front of the line looked at each other. They giggled nervously. Then they disappeared into the darkened gym.

Damont stuffed his hands into his pants pockets. "I've already been through this thing twice," he bragged.

"What did you win?" Sam asked.

Damont pulled coupons from one of his pockets. As he did, two pieces of popcorn and a gum wrapper fell from his pocket.

"Treats!" Wishbone quickly gobbled up the popcorn.

Damont waved his coupons in the air. "So far I get a free ice cream and a pencil." He broke into a grin. "But now I'm really good at getting through the maze. I'll be *two* times as fast as you."

The boy sitting at the door checked his watch. "Okay, you can go in now. But it's more fun if you go in alone."

"No problem." Damont handed his ticket over. He opened the gym door all the way. Loud music poured out. Then Damont disappeared into the dark opening.

"We're next!" Sam said as the door swung shut.

Wishbone sniffed the ground. "Yeah, but those pieces of popcorn made me hungry. Well, I'm almost always hungry, but now I'm *really* hungry. You might even say *starved*."

Wishbone's craving for food reminded him of the story "Hansel and Gretel." Hansel, a young boy, and his sister, Gretel, really *were* starving.

13

Wishbone here! "Hansel and Gretel" is one of many fairy tales that were written by the brothers Jacob and William Grimm. The stories were first written in Germany in the early 1800s. Around 1884 they were translated into English.

This story begins long, long ago in a house near a forest. That's where Hansel and his sister, Gretel, lived. Their father and their stepmother lived there, too. The children's father was a woodcutter. The family was so poor that they often had no food to eat. And Hansel and Gretel's stepmother was as mean as an alley cat. . . .

Chapter Two

Top Dog

Wishbone imagined himself as the boy, Hansel. His father was out of work. Food was running low again. Things seemed to get worse every day.

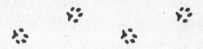

Hansel stood at his bedroom window in his family's small house. He rested his front paws on the window frame. The young boy stared out at the forest near his house. All he saw was green tree after green tree. There were so many trees, they did not let a lot of sunlight in. They made the forest always seem dark.

Hansel looked up at the sky. It was late in

the day. The stars were coming out. Soon it would be dark. "I'd be able to sleep better if my belly were full," Hansel said to his sister.

Across the room, Gretel lay on her bed. "Me, too." She huddled under a thin, ragged blanket to keep warm. As Hansel watched her, she finally fell asleep.

Poor Gretel. At least I'm not cold, Hansel thought. *I have this terrific fur coat to keep me warm!*

Hansel cocked his head. Voices drifted in from the next room. His sharp ears could pick up things Gretel wouldn't hear. And right at that moment he could hear every word his parents were saying—even the whispers.

"What are we going to do?" asked Hansel's father. "The food is almost gone. How can we feed the children? There isn't even enough food for the two of us!"

"There's only one thing *to* do," said Hansel's stepmother. "Tomorrow we'll give the kids each a slice of bread. Then we'll take the children deep into the forest with us. We'll start a fire to keep them warm."

Well, so far, so good, Hansel thought, as he listened carefully.

"Then . . ." said Stepmother, "we'll leave the children there by themselves. You and I will never return. They'll have to survive on their own."

"No!" Father shouted so loud that his words startled Gretel and woke her up.

The little girl sat up, rubbing the sleep from her eyes. "What's wrong?" she asked.

Hansel went over to her. Before he could say anything, Stepmother screeched. Hansel could hear her pacing the floor. "There's barely enough food for you and me. If we keep the children, we will *all* starve!"

"She wants to get rid of us!" Gretel said. Stepmother's voice had gotten so loud that Gretel could hear everything as well as Hansel did.

Hansel shook his head sadly.

"I cannot leave my children all alone in the woods!" Father shouted back. "The wild animals will eat them!"

"Whoa!" Hansel barked. Beside him, Gretel

17

shivered. Hansel knew it was because she was scared, not cold. "Go back to sleep. Everything will be okay." He wagged his tail slowly. *I hope!*

Gretel kept listening.

"You fool!" shouted Stepmother. She slammed a cupboard door. "If we keep the kids around, you may as well start building all our coffins!"

Father sighed but said nothing.

"Show her who's top dog, Dad!" Hansel said.

But no more words came from the room next door.

Hansel put a paw on his sister's shoulder. "Don't worry. I'll think of something."

Gretel fell back on the bed. "They're going to throw us out like old rags!"

Hansel continued to listen closely. When everyone else fell asleep, he crept to the front door. Quietly, he unhooked the latch of the door with his paw. Hansel stepped out into the cold, dark night.

Wishbone here. Hansel has a big problem on his paws—I mean *hands*.

In the meantime, let's see how things are moving along at Joe's school carnival.

Chapter Three

Twists and Turns

Wishbone sniffed the ticket taker. "How about you? Got any treats? Sweets? Meats? Junk food? I'm easy."

The big boy patted Wishbone's head. Then he looked at Sam, Joe, and David. They were still the only kids in line. He pointed at a poster. "You need to read the rules before you go in."

The puppy looked at the sign, too.

"'No food,'" Sam read.

Wishbone looked at Joe. "You said this carnival was going to be *fun!*"

"'No running,'" Sam read on. "'Stay on maze path.'" She shrugged her shoulders. "Those rules should be easy to follow."

"That's because *you're* not hungry," said Wishbone.

The boy sitting by the door held out his hand to David. "You can go in now."

David dropped his ticket into the boy's hand. "Here I go!" David opened the door and stepped into the dark gym. Music poured out the door.

"Hey! I hear birds, elephants, tigers—it's jungle music!" Wishbone wagged his tail. He was very curious about this game.

A minute later Sam entered the gym.

Finally, it was Joe's turn.

"I'm with him," Wishbone told the ticket taker. The puppy trotted beside Joe.

Just inside the gym, they stopped. Behind them, the door swung shut.

Wishbone jumped aside. "Hey! Watch the tail!"

The streak of daylight that had come through the doorway was suddenly gone. Wishbone waited for his eyes to get used to the darkness. Suddenly a round, dim light in the high ceiling flashed on. A split-second later it shut off. But Wishbone had already seen a few things.

The maze was made with cardboard boxes and chairs. Desks and tables lined the pathway, too. Some of the furniture had been tipped over onto its sides. And Sam was just ahead of them.

Wishbone sniffed. "Where's David?"

"Hey, where's David?" Joe slowly took a step forward.

"You're not listening, Joe," Wishbone said. "I just asked that!"

Wishbone heard a thump, like someone bumping into something.

"Joe! He's that way!" said the terrier. Wishbone leaped forward. He stopped when his leash pulled tight.

"Slow down, boy." Joe carefully felt his way along the different pieces of furniture. "It's really hard to see in here."

Wishbone tugged at the leash. "Can't, Joe. We'll never catch up to David."

"Hey!" Joe's hands flew up to his face. He was fighting something off.

"Watch out!" Wishbone barked. He jumped around, excited.

Then Joe laughed. "It's only balloons!" He swatted one away.

The light flashed. For an instant the gym was dimly lit. Joe and Wishbone were catching up to Sam. She was just up ahead. Wishbone looked around. He was now behind Joe. *Where is David?*

Wishbone spotted something small and yellow on the floor. He sniffed it. Then he wagged his tail. "Popcorn!" He gobbled down the treat in no time. "And there's another piece up near Sam!"

Wishbone headed for the tiny snack, but Joe pulled on the leash.

"Come on, Joe," Wishbone said. "I'll share with my best friend. . . ."

"Aargh!" Joe jumped. Surprised, Wishbone jumped, too. Something next to him also jumped. Wishbone jumped again.

Joe bent down and petted the puppy. "Sorry I scared you, boy. It's okay. That's just a mirror." He tapped it. "That's us you see."

"I knew that!" Wishbone stood tall.

The two walked forward slowly and rounded a corner. "Oops! A dead end, boy." Joe turned around. He felt his way back to the main path.

Wishbone remembered the piece of popcorn. He took the lead. "Follow me. Sam and my treat are just ahead." Wishbone zeroed in on the popcorn first.

"Sam!" Joe called, when the light flashed.

"Wait, Joe!" Wishbone said. "There's pop——" But it was too late. Joe led him away.

Joe hurried up to reach Sam. "Where's David?" he shouted over the loud and scary music.

Sam shrugged, then shouted. "I haven't seen him or Damont since I came in. Maybe they've made their way through the whole maze already."

Wishbone heard more sounds. He pricked up his ears. Scraping and bumping noises were coming from . . . uh . . . someone or some-*thing!* He barked. Joe didn't even look his way. Wishbone barked again. "Joe!" Joe still didn't pay any attention to the puppy. "Why won't you listen to me? I *always* listen to you."

Sam spun around. "Ugh!" She waved her arms wildly in the air. They got tangled in dangling strips of paper. She pushed her way past them.

Joe parted the strips and followed Sam. He laughed as the light flashed again.

"Oh!" Sam laughed, too, then shivered. "It felt like creepy things were crawling all over me."

"Like fleas? No, thank you!" Wishbone

belly-crawled *under* the strips so none touched him.

Joe, along with Wishbone, stepped ahead of Sam. Joe felt his way along the maze. Wishbone walked with his nose to the floor. "Popcorn, popcorn, popcorn—"

"Whoa!" Joe's arm flew up and covered his eyes. Laughing, he twisted away from a wall. "Look out for the blast of air, Sam!" But it was too late.

"Oh!" Sam spun as the blast of air hit her face and hair. Giggling, she shook her ponytail back into place.

"I hardly felt a thing," Wishbone said. "And *my* hair didn't get messed up."

Suddenly the floor vibrated under the puppy's paws.

"Joe! Joe! Something is up ahead and that way." Wishbone pointed left with his nose. "Maybe we should go the other way. I'm not sure *why*, exactly. I just have a feeling. . . ."

The light flashed again.

"Hey!" Wishbone saw someone's leg disappear into the dark maze ahead and to the right. He barked. "Let's follow him—or her. Maybe we'll get out of here."

But Joe tugged him to the left. A few steps later, they turned.

"This is the way we're *not* supposed to go, Joe." Wishbone planted his four paws on the floor and steadied himself.

"Come on, Wishbone," Joe called.

Wishbone held his ground. "I don't think we should." He was straining to keep Joe from going the wrong way.

But with the next flash of light, Wishbone changed his mind. They were in a far corner of

27

the gym. Through a doorway, Wishbone could see wire bins. And they were filled with balls. Baseballs! Basketballs! Soccer balls! Wishbone wagged his tail. He hurried through the doorway with Joe and Sam.

Then the door slammed behind them.

Sam and Joe spun around. The fur on Wishbone's back stood up.

"What's going on?" Sam asked over the music.

Wishbone cocked his head and listened. Something heavy was being shoved against the other side of the door.

The terrier sniffed the door. Then he scratched at it. "Some*one* or some*thing* is blocking us in!"

Wishbone here. Whew! That last turn turned into quite a big surprise. A bad one!

Let's go and see if Hansel and Gretel are having any better luck.

Chapter Four

Crumbs

Hansel closed the door behind him. The moon was full and bright.

"I've got to find a way to save my sister and me!"

Hansel sniffed his way across the yard. He sniffed his way back to the house. White pebbles lay on the dirt where he'd dug holes. He had been digging earlier in the day. In the moonlight, the rocks glittered like small silver coins.

"That's it!" He wagged his tail. "These pebbles will be a big help!" He quickly filled his pockets with them.

Hansel crept back inside and went to sleep. He dreamed of a giant, meaty bone.

"Get up, you lazybones!"

Hansel jumped up on all fours from a sound sleep. It was still dark outside. He knew the voice he'd heard belonged to Stepmother. Hansel could see her shape through the darkness. She stood with her hands on her hips, watching the kids. Hansel growled too softly for her to hear. *But growling sure makes me feel better!* he thought.

Gretel hurried over to his side.

Hansel smelled . . . what was it? Fear . . . Yes, that was it! *Poor Gretel!* he thought.

"We're all going into the forest to look for wood." Stepmother held out her hands. "This is for your dinner. Do not eat it before then. If you do, you'll get nothing else!"

Hansel sniffed Stepmother's hands. A small piece of bread was in each. Gretel took one piece. Hansel took the other in his mouth.

"Come! Don't take so long." Stepmother hurried out of the room.

Gretel's shoulder's drooped. "Stepmother is so mean!" The girl put her piece of bread into the apron pocket of her shabby dress.

"Carry mine, too," Hansel whispered.

When Gretel opened her apron pocket again, Hansel dropped his bread in. "Don't worry about Stepmother's plan." He patted the pebbles in his pockets. "I have a plan of my own!"

"Get out here right now!" Stepmother ordered.

Gretel put on her coat. Hansel trotted out of the room, with his sister right behind him.

Father and Stepmother stood by the front door.

"Good morning, children," Father said.

"Yes, it is!" Hansel wagged his tail. He was all ready for Stepmother's evil trick. *And I'm pretty good at knowing what to do when it comes to tricks, too,* Hansel thought.

It was almost light when the family stepped outside. A chilly wind blew at their backs. Gretel shivered. Hansel walked along with everyone for a while. Then he slowed down. When no one was looking, he dropped a pebble from his pocket onto the cold, hard ground. Then, as he trotted ahead, he glanced back at it and wagged his tail happily.

Gretel turned and gave her brother a surprised look.

You'll see, Hansel's eyes told her. Then he trotted on, dropping more white pebbles as he went.

When everyone had walked a long way into the thick forest, Father and Stepmother suddenly stopped.

Father pointed at the sticks on the ground. "Children, gather some twigs. I'll make a nice fire to keep you warm."

Hansel trotted around. His long, narrow mouth was perfect for picking up branches. Soon he and Gretel had a big pile to burn.

Father rubbed two sticks together. Hansel smelled smoke. A minute later yellow flames licked at the air. Then Father added a big log to the fire.

"Husband and I will go farther into the forest to cut wood," Stepmother said. "We'll come back for you when we're done." She smiled at the children and left.

Yeah, right! Hansel thought. But aloud he said, "Yes, Stepmother."

Father brushed away a tear as he left.

Hansel and Gretel sat down on the ground in front of the fire. Gretel pulled out the bread pieces from her apron pocket. It was almost noon. "I'm going to eat now," she said. "I'm too hungry to wait until dinner."

"Me, too." Hansel licked his chops.

Gretel handed him his bread.

Hansel gulped it down. The heat from the fire made him sleepy. He lay down. Gretel lay down, too. Not far away, the steady thumping of Father's axe lulled them to sleep.

Hansel awoke with a start. It was dark and very cold. Gretel was shaking him. "We're all alone! How are we going to get home?" She cried.

Hansel licked her hand. "Wait until the moon rises, Gretel. Then we'll be able to find our way."

The young boy stood and stretched. Hansel wandered around the area and checked out some of the trees. Then he trotted back to his sister.

"The moon is up." He used his nose to point at the white pebbles. They were all scattered in a line along the ground. "Look, Gretel. I dropped the white pebbles along the way. They should help us find our way home."

"They shine like silver coins!" Gretel hugged his neck. "You're a genius, Hansel!"

"Thanks, Gretel," Hansel barked. "It's in my blood."

Hansel and Gretel followed the trail of shining white pebbles. Finally, they left the darkness of the forest. They reached home just as daylight lit up the sky.

Hansel scratched on the door.

Stepmother opened it. "Oh!" She looked surprised, then angry. "You've been very bad children! Why did you sleep for so long in the forest? We were worried you would never come home!"

Worried? Ha! Hansel thought.

"But—" Gretel hushed as the door opened wider. "Father!" she cried.

"Children!" Father opened his arms wide. "I'm so glad to see you."

Hansel knew his father was telling the truth. Hansel, Gretel, and their father hugged one another.

"Why did you leave us all alone in the forest?" Gretel finally asked.

"It was a mistake," Father said. Then he hugged his two children again. They all went inside.

All day, Father hugged the two children whenever he saw them. Stepmother gave them only angry looks. She said nothing. But that night, while Gretel slept, Hansel heard Stepmother say plenty.

Hansel didn't want to hear Stepmother's ugly words. He lay on his bedroom floor and chewed noisily on a stick. *It's a meaty bone. It's a meaty bone. It's a meaty bone,* he told himself.

Still he could hear Stepmother. She said, "We'll take them even farther into the forest tomorrow. We'll go so deep into the woods that they'll never find their way home!" She laughed.

Hansel listened for his father's reply.

"Yes, Wife." His father sighed. Hansel could hear the sadness in his father's voice.

Here we go again, Hansel thought. *Father sure isn't acting like the top dog now. I'll need to pick up more pebbles tonight.*

Time seemed to fly by. Soon it was dark

outside. Moonlight streamed in through the children's bedroom window. Hansel kept chewing on his stick. After a while, all was quiet in the next room. He crept to the front door.

Standing up on two legs, Hansel pawed the door latch. The latch swung free, but the door wouldn't open.

Hmm . . . Hansel eyed the door. Above the latch was a bolt. It was locked! Hansel stretched higher. *I—can't—reach—it!* He jumped up, then landed hard on the wood floor with a thump. *Shh!* he told himself. He stretched as high as he could. He still couldn't reach the bolt.

Sighing, Hansel gave up and went to bed. He slept. He dreamed of a food bowl the size of the moon. It was filled with a rich beef stew. In the stew was a giant, meaty bone.

"Get up!"

Stepmother's booming voice startled Hansel and woke him up right away. He bounded up from his bed to all four paws. He heard Gretel jump to her feet.

"It's time to go out to the forest again." Stepmother threw Gretel her coat. Then she shooed Hansel and Gretel out of the bedroom.

"She sure gets up on the wrong side of the bed a lot," Hansel whispered to his sister.

Father waited for them by the front door. He had a sad look in his eyes.

"Here." Stepmother shoved a dry biscuit into Gretel's hand. "Save this for later. You and your brother will have to share it." Then the woman grabbed Father by his coat sleeve. They stepped outside of their run-down house.

Gretel dropped the biscuit into her apron pocket. "I don't think there *is* a right side to her bed!" she whispered to her brother.

Hansel nodded as he and Gretel followed their parents into the forest. The old biscuit smelled good. Hansel was hungry enough to eat cat food! Then he remembered why they were going into the woods again. To be left behind! And he didn't have a single pebble to make a path.

Hansel walked slower than the others. "Pssst! Gretel!"

Gretel waited for him to catch up.

"I need my half of the biscuit," Hansel whispered. "I don't have any pebbles to make a trail."

"What!" Gretel stared at him wide-eyed. "Oh, okay." Then she took out the biscuit and broke it in two.

"Thanks." Hansel took his piece with his teeth and trotted on. Oh, how he wanted to chomp down on the biscuit! Any food, even stale, would be welcome. He was so tired of being hungry. Just one big crunch and his belly would stop aching.

Instead, Hansel gently gnawed the biscuit. He ground it up carefully between his teeth. He spat out a crumb. A little farther on, he did the same thing again. He stopped and looked down. Another crumb lay on the ground. His plan was working. He was leaving a trail to follow home later!

"What are you looking at?" Stepmother said, as she slowed down to watch the boy.

I'm always in her doghouse! Glancing back, Hansel spotted a crow. "I was just waving to that bird."

"Stop wasting time!"

"Yes, Stepmother." Hansel smiled at Gretel. Then he followed his parents. Everyone walked for a long time without talking. The only sounds around were those made by the birds. There sure seemed to be a lot of them flying around!

Hansel's piece of biscuit was gone just as his parents stopped to make a fire. *Perfect!* he

thought. He licked the last few crumbs from his muzzle.

Hansel sniffed the air. Then he sniffed the ground. *I've never gone this deep into the woods before. Nothing around here smells familiar.*

"Sit!" Stepmother said sharply.

Hansel dropped quickly. He yawned.

Stepmother tossed a few branches onto the fire. "Stay here. Your father and I are going deeper into the forest to cut wood. When we're finished, we'll come fetch you."

"Right." Hansel and Gretel exchanged knowing looks.

"Good-bye," Father said sadly.

Stepmother pulled Father away. They disappeared into the thick growth of trees.

Brother and sister shared Gretel's biscuit. It was tasty. Hansel dropped to his belly. Soaking up the heat from the fire, he fell asleep.

When Hansel awoke later, Gretel was sleeping. "Nap time's over!" Hansel licked her cheek gently. "The moon's up, Gretel. We can start home now."

Gretel sat up slowly. She looked on the ground around her and frowned. "Where's our trail?"

Hansel followed her gaze. The bread crumbs he'd left didn't catch the light of the moon the way the white pebbles had. It was a good thing Hansel had such a terrific nose. He'd sniff his way from crumb to crumb. "Don't worry, Gretel. I'll find the biscuit crumbs. We'll get home."

Hansel went to work. He put his nose to the ground. Step . . . sniff. Step . . . sniff. Hansel's head popped up. *Nothing!*

"Oh! Now I know why all those birds followed us. They were eating the bread crumbs. Gretel, our trail is gone!"

Gretel gasped. "How are we going to get back home?"

Hansel howled. "I don't know. . . ."

Chapter Five

Treats and More Treats

*G*retel and I are in deep trouble, Hansel thought. He stared into the endless darkness. The forest was like a big cage around them—a cage without a door. It was keeping them from getting home!

Suddenly, a loud roar broke the silence in the woods.

Hansel's fur bristled. *Danger!* He looked into the blackness and growled.

"Hansel, I'm scared!" Gretel reached out and grabbed him.

Whatever cat made that roar sounds bigger than any I have ever chased! Hansel put a paw on his sister's arm. He tried to comfort her. "Come, Gretel!"

They walked away quietly. They walked all night. When the sun finally rose, they were still in the forest.

"Maybe we're walking in circles," Gretel groaned.

Hansel sniffed some trees. Then he wagged his tail. "We haven't been *here*."

Hansel stretched. He was very tired. Gretel was walking slower and slower. She could hardly move her feet. He and his sister were both weak from hunger.

"Let's see if we can dig up something to eat," Hansel said.

The two walked on. Finally, Gretel pointed to a bush. "Berries!" she exclaimed, as Hansel followed her finger.

Hansel stayed at her heels. He and Gretel quickly reached the berry bushes.

Hansel picked a red berry with his teeth. "Do these come in bigger sizes? . . . How about different flavors? Beef? Chicken?"

A flash of white streaked past Hansel.

"A bird!" Hansel raced after it, barking.

Giggling, Gretel followed him.

"Look!" Hansel stopped in his tracks.

The bird landed on the roof of a tiny house.

Hansel took a couple of deep sniffs. "Wow! The house is made of gingerbread." He wagged his tail happily. "My idea of a dream come true!"

Gretel pointed up. "The roof is made of cookies and gumdrops. And the chimney is made of chocolate-covered almonds." She ran to a window and nibbled. "These window-panes are made of banana, cherry, lime, and grape lollipops!"

"Snack time!" Hansel jumped onto a tree stump, then up to a barrel that stood against the house. Standing on his back paws and stretching up, he pulled a cookie off the roof. "*Oatmeal!* My favorite."

From inside the house came a soft voice:

> *Nibble, nibble, like a mouse,*
> *Who is nibbling at my house?*

"Did you hear that?" Hansel asked.

Gretel whispered, "It's only the wind."

Hansel tore off a big piece of the roof. He jumped down next to Gretel and gobbled down the tasty treat.

The door of the cottage creaked open slowly. A skinny old woman came outside limping. She used a walking stick. At first she didn't look at the children. She raised her long, pointy nose and sniffed the air. Then, slowly, she turned her head their way. "Oh, hello, children." She grinned. Her lips were cracked. Some of her teeth were broken. Others were missing.

Boy, it looks as if she's been eating too many of the treats around the house! Hansel thought.

"Hello," they answered together.

The woman came near them. They backed away. She came closer. Bending, she put her face close to Hansel's. "Oh, a boy!"

Wow! Hansel stepped back. The old woman's breath smelled like rotten fish. He shivered as he looked into her beady red eyes. *Boy, if she's got to get that close, she must have really bad eyesight!*

The old woman turned. She put her nose

right up to Gretel's. Gretel trembled. "And a girl, too! How nice. Are you children hungry?"

Gretel mumbled, "I'm starving!"

Hansel agreed. *There is something odd about this old woman,* thought Hansel. But he was so hungry, all he could think about was food.

"Poor children. Come inside with me. No harm will come to you at my house." She took Gretel by the hand. They walked toward the front door. "I'll make you pancakes. After you eat, I'll give you a nice, soft place to rest."

Hansel wagged his tail. *Pancakes! Yummy!*

Uh . . . not to be greedy or anything . . . but how about something with a little more bite to it—like, say, a breakfast steak?

Suddenly, Hansel saw that Gretel and the old woman were going inside. He ran.

"Hey, wait for me!" he called.

The front room was clean and cozy. A picture hung on one wall. The words on it said: HOME, SWEET HOME.

"I'll say it's sweet! I've already tasted a few samples," Hansel said. A comfortable-looking pink sofa was underneath the picture. Hansel put his nose to the floor. *Not one crumb! Darn!* He sniffed his way to the kitchen. One corner was stacked high with crates, tins, and wooden boxes. In another corner stood a big black cooking stove.

"Warm yourselves by the stove, children." The old woman began to make them a meal.

"Don't mind if I do!" Hansel said. *This woman isn't so bad.*

Gretel smiled at Hansel. She took off her coat and held her hands near the stove. "Oh, this feels so good."

Soon the food was ready.

Gretel sat on a stool at the table. Hansel made himself at home, curling up on the floor in front of the stove.

The woman eyed them carefully. "The two of you are much too thin. How many pancakes would you like?"

Hansel wagged his tail. *Does the phrase* SUPER SIZE IT *mean anything to you?*

The woman grinned. She gave both of them a plate with three fluffy pancakes. Hansel got up and sat across from his sister. The woman set another stack of pancakes between the two children.

"Thank you!" Hansel gulped down his food at top speed. Soon every piece was gone. "That was *so* good." Hansel licked his plate.

"I am *really* full." Gretel sighed happily. "Doesn't it feel great?"

Hansel wagged his tail. "I'll let you know in a minute!" He gulped down the rest of the pancakes the woman had set on the table. He burped, then yawned. "I'm very sleepy."

"Me, too." Gretel yawned.

"Come." The old woman led them to a cheerful-looking room. In it were two beds.

Gretel chose the one near the window. She got in bed and then tucked herself under the thick blanket. "This bed is so soft."

Hansel jumped up onto the other bed. He circled twice, then lay down. His eyes were closing fast.

"Rest, child." The old woman's cold hands squeezed Hansel's front leg. Hansel shivered. "You are all bones. You must eat more." She bent closer to his ear. "I'll have a big surprise waiting for you when you wake up." She let out a high-pitched laugh, then left the room.

Hansel shivered again. Something was wrong. Was he dreaming already? Or did he smell *danger?* He wasn't sure. But only witches laughed in that high-pitched way. *Get away from here!* a voice inside his head told him. But Hansel was too tired to follow his own command. His eyelids felt heavy. They closed tightly as he fell into a deep sleep.

Chapter Six

Adding Up

"Hey!" Hansel awoke to someone pulling on his shirt collar. It was dark. He could not see. But he could *smell* the old woman. Hansel tried to twist free of her firm grip. But the woman was as strong as a sheep dog. She dragged the small boy out of bed.

"I don't like big surprises. Really! Can't we talk about this?" Hansel tried to dig his nails into the wood floor.

"But I *love* surprises!" The old woman laughed. She dragged him into the kitchen. And she had no limp!

The roaring fire in the big stove made the room glow. Hansel's fur bristled. The boxes and tins in the corner were gone. In their place was a cage! It had strong wooden bars, with spaces between them. Hansel glanced at the woman. *That's it! Poor eyesight . . . beady red eyes . . . a nose as well trained as any dog's. Those add up to one thing—she's a witch!*

"Surprise!" The witch laughed again. She kicked poor Hansel through the opened door into the cage.

Hansel landed on a dirty, ragged blanket. He jumped to all fours. Before he could run out, the witch slammed the door shut. She locked it with a heavy piece of wood.

Hansel stared out between the bars. He was scared.

Gretel ran into the kitchen. "What's all the noise? What are you doing to my brother? Why is he locked in that cage?"

"I'm going to fatten him up."

"Run, Gretel!" Hansel barked. "She's a witch! She tricked us with her sweet house! I bet she has done this to other children."

"Oh, no!" Gretel took a step back.

The witch let out one of her horrible laughs. "And where would you run *to?* Deeper

into the forest? No. That would be much too scary for a child alone. Other children have tried to escape from me. I always catch them." She pointed a finger at Gretel. "You, my little girl, will cook his food." She bent down and put her dried-up face close to Hansel's muzzle. "And you, my boy, will be a fine Saturday supper for me."

Helllooo! Hansel thought. *I don't think so!*

Gretel started to cry.

"Hush, girl!" the witch cried. She glared at Gretel. "You have a lot to do before Saturday. Fetch some water. Then cook a nice big stew for your brother." She stuck a pail in Gretel's hand and pushed her out the back door. "Get to work—and fast!" the witch demanded.

Hansel barked.

The witch turned around, angry. "What is it?" she snapped.

"What day is this?" Hansel asked, sitting in the cage.

"Thursday. Why does it matter to you?" The witch's face looked as hard as stone.

Hansel rubbed a paw over one eye. *In two*

days I'll be . . . a hot dog! Unless . . . Hansel pulled himself up. "You know, I'm not all that tasty. In fact, I'm really tough!" He growled loudly. *In more ways than one!* he thought.

The witch gave an ear-splitting laugh. She turned around and grabbed Gretel. Gretel was just bringing in water from the well in the yard. "Hurry, girl. Your brother needs fattening up. I'm getting *very* hungry."

Gretel's eyes filled with tears. "I want to go home."

Hansel stretched a paw through the bars. He couldn't reach Gretel.

"Make him a stew of chicken with dumplings," the witch ordered. She showed Gretel a big iron pot. "I'll be watching every move you make."

Hansel lay down. Soon he smelled the aroma of chicken boiling. Hansel turned to watch his sister through the bars of the cage door. A little while later Gretel brought a big bowl of food to the cage.

"Get back, boy!" the witch yelled. She scraped a stick across the bars of the cage door.

Hansel jumped back.

The witch opened the door slowly. "Slide it in, girl—and be quick about it!" she ordered Gretel.

Any other day, Hansel would have loved to smell such food. *But right now I have more important things on my mind. Like how* not *to be Saturday night's supper!*

The witch banged the cage door shut and locked it. "Eat up, boy!" she said with a wicked laugh. Then she turned to Gretel. She pointed a long, crooked finger at her. "You get crab shells to eat. When you're done, I have plenty more work for you to do."

Hansel stopped eating. "I'll share with Gretel."

The witch glared at him. Her beady red eyes seemed to burn right through him. "If you give her even *one crumb,* you'll never see her again."

Hansel growled, then went back to eating. At the bottom of his bowl was a bone.

Hmm . . . Something made him want to keep the bone. Hansel walked to the back of

the cage. He pushed the bone under the edge of his blanket.

Hansel paced. Gretel dragged in another pailful of water. She washed the dishes. She carried in piles of wood to keep the oven burning. Then the witch made her cook more food.

She's working Gretel to the bone! Hansel thought. Then he thought about what was to happen to him. Nervously, he began to chew on the wooden bars of his cage.

"Stop that chewing!" cried the witch.

Hansel looked up, startled. *I guess she has the same "no chewing" rules that we have at home.*

Later, the witch commanded, "Set another bowl in his cage."

"I'm sorry for all the food," Gretel whispered to Hansel. "Please don't get fat." The witch pushed Gretel away.

Hansel sniffed at the food. He couldn't believe it! He was *not* hungry.

"Eat!" the witch ordered.

Hansel ate. When he finished, the witch held up a cup of water. "Would you like a drink?"

Hansel eyed the cup. He wanted to tell the witch "no!" and turn his tail to her. But he was very thirsty. "Yes," he said softly.

"First, give me your arm." The witch squinted at him. She held out her bony hand. "Now, let's see if those meals have plumped you up."

He had eaten a lot. His body *felt* heavy. *What if I'm getting fat already?* Then Hansel thought about the witch's bad eyesight. *The bone!* he thought. *I'll use the bone!* He quickly

61

dug out the chicken bone and held it between the bars.

The witch felt it. "You're still too thin!" She opened the door and put the cup inside his cage. Then she closed it, locked it, and turned away.

Hansel hid the bone. *I tricked her!* He was so happy he wanted to flip in the air. As he lapped up the cool water, he heard the witch give another order.

"Gretel! Make more food!" she demanded.

Wishbone here. The clock is ticking away for poor Hansel. Saturday is getting closer by the second!

Let's see what kind of a time they're having in Oakdale.

Chapter Seven

Tricks

Wishbone realized that he and his friends had been locked in a large closet. Before his eyes got used to the darkness, Joe found a light switch and flipped it on. Wishbone looked at the wire bins against one wall. "So *this* is where the school hides all of the balls! Hey—what's in the big box over in that corner?"

"We've been tricked!" Joe told Sam. "Someone changed the direction of the maze to get us into this storage closet."

Wishbone cocked his head to one side. "I can hear scraping sounds. I think it must be more furniture being moved outside the door." He sniffed. "I smell Damont!"

Sam tried to open the door. Then she pushed against it with her shoulder. "It won't open. Do you think Damont did this?"

Wishbone sighed. "Nobody listens to the puppy. I just *know* they'll listen to me when I'm fully grown!"

Suddenly Wishbone heard Damont laugh. "I'll be back!" Damont yelled over the music. "But *not* to let you out."

"Damont!" Sam and Joe called. Together they pushed on the door. It wouldn't budge.

Sam sighed. "I wonder when he's going to let us out."

Wishbone heard more scraping. "I think Damont is changing the maze back to the way it's supposed to be."

"If we bang on the door, maybe someone will hear us." Joe began to beat on the door with his fists.

Sam pounded, too. "Help!" she yelled. "We're locked in the closet!"

"Let us out!" Joe banged harder.

Wishbone barked. "Joe, Sam! *Listen* to me. Damont changed the maze back to the way it

64

was before. No one will get close enough to the closet to hear you."

Joe rubbed his hands. "We need a plan."

"You're right," Sam said. "Maybe we just have to think hard."

"Okay." Joe paced one way, Sam paced the other.

"Dog coming through." Wishbone cut across their paths.

"Hey! I've got an idea!" Joe shook a finger in the air. "Damont *really* wants to win Space Jumpers. What if we tell him *we* have it?"

"You mean *pretend* we have the game?" Sam asked.

Joe looked around. "Let's see what's in this box." He dug through it. "Jump ropes, mitts, and balls. If we can get Damont to look in here, maybe we can escape."

"And go get a snack, too, right?" Wishbone wagged his tail.

"Trick him the way he tricked us." Sam smiled. "We just have to wait for Damont to come back."

The puppy stretched to see inside the box.

"Could one of you reach in and get me a rope? I'm ready for a good chew." He looked at Joe and Sam. "No?"

"I guess I can take Wishbone's leash off for a while. None of us is going anywhere." Joe bent down and took it off.

"That works. Thank you!"

Wishbone lay down near the door to wait. He didn't wait long.

"Someone's outside the door!" he told the kids.

"Hey!" Damont yelled over the music. "You still in there?"

"Shh!" Joe put his finger to his lips. He and Sam had their backs to the door. They faced the box.

"I *know* you're in there," Damont said. "All the furniture is still piled up against the door."

Wishbone, Joe, and Sam didn't make a sound.

"Hey! Don't you want to get out of there?" Damont asked.

No answer.

Wishbone heard furniture being pushed away. "Joe, the plan's working!" He stood up.

As the closet door opened, Joe and Sam spun around.

"Damont!" Joe and Sam tried to sound as if they were surprised.

"Why didn't you answer me?" Damont asked.

"We were busy," Joe said.

"Me, too," Wishbone barked.

"Doing what?" Damont eyed them with suspicion. "You don't want to come out of here? You don't want to win Space Jumpers?"

Joe and Sam exchanged looks.

"Come on!" Damont narrowed his eyes. "I don't have all day."

"We already have—" Sam stopped. She quickly glanced at the box behind her.

"Sam!" Joe frowned at her. "Don't tell him!"

Wishbone wagged his tail. "You two can really act!"

"Tell me *what?*" Damont looked around them. "You two are hiding something. I bet

the game is in that box!" Damont pushed his way between them.

Joe, Sam, and Wishbone raced out of the storage closet.

Joe slammed the door. As he turned to run, he bumped into a table. It scraped across the floor.

"I'd better feel my way around," Joe said, walking very slowly and carefully. "Until my eyes get used to the dark."

The maze light flashed on, then off.

"This way, Joe!" Sam called.

"Hey, you guys! Let me out of here!" Now it was Damont's turn to bang on the door.

"Is it just me, or does he sound angry?" Wishbone scooted behind the kids.

Joe felt his way along in the dark. "Now let's find the real maze path."

"It's good to be free." Wishbone slowed to sniff a chair seat. "Free from the leash—*and* free from the closet."

Hi! Wishbone here. Freeing yourself from a closet is one thing. But freeing yourself from a witch—now, that's a different story! Let's see how Hansel and Gretel are handling things.

Chapter Eight

Top Dog of Tricks

By Saturday afternoon Hansel had eaten enough food for a whole family. And he really needed some exercise.

Hansel looked out between the wooden bars of his cage. Gretel was adding a log to the fire in the stove. *Wow! She's strong. It must be all those crab shells she's eating.*

The witch came near Hansel's cage. "Let me feel your arm."

He dug out the chicken bone from under his blanket. He held it up. The witch leaned so close that Hansel could smell her breath. *Fishy as a cat's!*

The witch pinched the bone. "Too thin! Stick out your leg."

Hansel moved the chicken bone between two other bars.

The witch poked it. "You're skinny as a skeleton. But I'll wait no longer!" The witch pushed away the piece of wood that kept the cage door locked. She reached in for Hansel. "Your sister has a nice, hot fire burning in the oven."

"But I'm not cold!" Hansel backed away from the witch's hand. "Honest."

The witch stretched. Her long, cold fingers grabbed Hansel's collar. She pulled.

"I don't think so!" Hansel pulled back. But the witch pulled harder. She yanked Hansel out of the cage.

Letting out an evil laugh, she pinned him under one arm.

Hansel noticed something different about the witch's teeth. He hadn't noticed it before. They were long and pointed. *Boy, she'd make a dentist rich!*

I need a plan. Fast! If I want to save this cute little furred neck of mine! Hansel kicked his back legs and tried to break free.

The witch squeezed him tight.

Gretel ran over and pulled on the witch's arm. "Let my brother go!"

"You silly mouse!" The old witch grabbed Gretel with her other hand.

Hansel felt the heat as they got near the oven. But he shivered. He and Gretel were in real danger. *I have to do something, or I'll become a crispy critter. But what can I do?*

"Open the oven door!" The witch pushed Gretel forward.

Gretel's hands shook. She removed the metal bar that was placed across the oven door. She then pulled open the heavy door until the oven looked like a huge mouth.

The witch grinned slyly at Gretel. "Now crawl in, child, and see if the oven is hot enough."

"No way!" Gretel cried.

Hansel exchanged looks with his sister. *The witch is trying to trick Gretel! She plans to cook us both! Well, I'll show her who's the top dog of tricks.*

Hansel tilted his head one way, then the

other. He pretended to check out the oven. "You know, I bet there isn't room in there for both of us at once."

The witch frowned. "Of course there is, you silly fool!" she cried. "I'm much bigger than the two of you put together. And look!" The witch let go of Hansel. He dropped to the floor. Then the wicked witch leaned into the oven as far as her waist.

Vivian Sathre

And you think I'm *a silly fool?* Hansel jumped at the oven door. The witch lost her balance. She tumbled all the way into the burning-hot oven.

The door slammed shut. Gretel dropped the metal bar across the door, trapping the witch inside.

Suddenly the oven hissed as if it were a giant cat. Then it spat angry black smoke. The witch screeched.

"I am outta here!" Hansel ran out of the kitchen. Gretel was right beside him.

Chapter Nine

Cleaning Up

When it was quiet again, Hansel trotted back to the kitchen. He peeked into the room. The fire in the stove burned gently.

"We did it, Gretel!" Hansel howled.

Gretel came over and hugged his furred neck. "We're free! Free of the witch!" She ran into the kitchen. She grabbed an apple, bread, and cheese. She gobbled some of each as she joined Hansel again.

Hansel looked around the front room. It still had the picture with the sign that said HOME, SWEET HOME. And the sofa was there, too. But now the tins, boxes, and crates from the kitchen were in the front room, too. "I wonder what's in those." Hansel went over and nosed open a box. "It's filled with jewels, Gretel! Bright, red jewels." Hansel wagged his tail. "They're beautiful, even if we can't eat them."

Gretel pulled the lid off one of the metal tins. "More jewels!"

Hansel and Gretel filled their pockets with the glittering gems.

"Now we have to find our way out of the forest," Hansel said.

Gretel grabbed her coat and more food.

The two children went outside. Jumping high, Hansel licked a window. "Not bad. There's even a little dirt on it. Very tasty." Then he and Gretel walked into the forest.

Trees, trees, and more trees! Hansel raced ahead. Then he ran back to Gretel.

Hansel pointed with his nose. "I think we should go this way." *I'm not sure why*, he thought, as he and Gretel ran among the trees. I just have a feeling. . . .

They ran and ran. Finally, Hansel stopped and panted. He saw a stick on the ground in front of him. Some of its bark was missing.

"Hey, I'd recognize those teeth marks

anywhere. They're mine!" He sniffed around. "And these are my trees." Hansel wagged his tail. "Gretel, I know exactly where we are. We're almost home. Come on!"

They ran.

With every step, Hansel imagined that he could see his father. He could hardly wait to hug him.

"I can see the house now!" Hansel ran faster. When he reached the yard, he barked with joy. "Helllooo!"

The door flew open. There stood Father. His arms were open wide. "My children!"

"Group hug!" Hansel called out. He and Gretel rushed into Father's waiting arms.

Hansel licked Father's face.

"I'm so happy to see you!" Tears ran down Father's cheeks. He gave a playful scratch to Hansel's ear. He kissed Gretel's cheek. "I thought I'd never see you again."

"Is Stepmother still mean to the bone?" Hansel asked.

Father shook his head. "She's dead. She choked on the last piece of stale bread."

"We have a surprise for you, Father."
Hansel wagged his tail with glee. Then he
opened his pockets wide.

Father gasped. "Jewels!"

"We'll never starve again, Father!" Gretel
cried. She opened her apron pocket. "Look—
more jewels! We can trade these for anything
we want."

"*I* want toys." Hansel scratched his side.
"You know, something besides sticks and
old leather shoes that I can really sink my
teeth into."

"Oh, my dear children!" Father said. "All
our worries are gone. And it's thanks to you!"
Smiling, he took Gretel by the hands. They
danced in a circle.

Hansel was so happy he flipped in the air.
One of the jewels fell from his pocket. He
picked it up with his teeth. "I think I'll bury
the jewels now—just to keep them safe."

Hansel trotted behind the house. He
found a good spot and started to dig.

"Dirt to dig in. Grass to roll in. And more
than enough jewels to buy a whole butcher

shop." Hansel smiled. He sighed with a feeling of happiness. "Home, sweet home!"

Wishbone here! Hansel and Gretel are safe at home.
Let's see if the Oakdale gang is out of the woods yet.

Chapter Ten

Cute Little Puppy Cleanup

The puppy trotted on through the maze. He was ahead of Joe and Sam. Wishbone could still hear Damont banging on the closet door. But the farther away he got, the softer the banging became. "Joe, Sam! I found the right path!"

The light flashed.

"And there's a piece of popcorn." Wishbone gobbled it down.

"There he is!" Joe said, pointing at Wishbone. "He's eating something off the floor."

Joe and Sam made their way to Wishbone.

"Wishbone, you found the path for us!" Sam said.

The puppy looked up at her. "Didn't I just

say that?" He wagged his tail proudly. "Follow me." He trotted on. "Hey, here's another piece of popcorn! Now you see it . . ." His tongue struck as the light flashed on. ". . . and now you don't!"

"That *something* he's eating is popcorn," Sam said.

Joe pointed past Wishbone. "I saw a door over there when the light just flashed."

Sam and Joe quickly felt their way up to Wishbone.

Wishbone kept finding bits and pieces of popcorn every few steps.

"Where did all this popcorn come from?" Sam asked, as her feet kept crunching on scraps of it.

"I've been wondering that, too," Joe said. "Here's the door! And the pieces of popcorn led right to it!"

Joe pushed the metal bar on the door. The door opened.

"We're free!" Wishbone ran through the doorway. He was outside the gym. He blinked his eyes against the daylight.

Joe and Sam were right behind the terrier. Hurrying toward them was David.

"David! David! David!" The happy puppy greeted his friend with jumps and flips.

"We're glad to see you!" Sam smiled.

"Yeah," Joe said.

"Where were you for so long?" David asked. "You never came out."

"Damont locked us in the storage closet." Joe kneeled down. He scratched Wishbone behind the ears.

Sam smiled. "But we tricked him into letting us out."

David listened while Joe explained.

"You forgot to tell him that I cleaned up the popcorn trail." Wishbone wagged his tail. "There is no job too big for the cute little puppy."

"Hey!" a voice called out from behind them. "Aren't you going to draw for a prize?"

Wishbone turned his head and looked over his tail. Sitting on the ground by the gym door was a girl. She was holding a big box in her lap.

David held up his coupon. "I won a pack of gum."

Joe nodded. "You go first, Sam."

"Thanks." Sam walked over to the box. She stuck her hand in and pulled out a coupon. She smiled. "I win a half hour with one of the school computers."

Joe reached in. He dug around, then pulled out a coupon. "I can't believe it!" He grinned. "I won the Space Jumpers! game!"

Wishbone tried to do his best flip. "Way to go, buddy!"

Sam and David gave each other a high-five. David slapped Joe on the back.

"You guys locked me in!"

Wishbone and the kids spun around.

Damont was standing by the gym door. He looked as angry as a wet cat.

Joe shook his head. "All I did was shut the closet door. I didn't lock you in."

Damont stuck out his chin. "B-but I *thought* you locked me in. And then someone picked up my—" Damont stopped.

"And then someone picked up your what?" Sam asked.

"Forget it," Damont said.

Wishbone sniffed near Damont's pockets. "Aha! Popcorn! Here's your maze litterbug!"

Damont eyed the puppy with suspicion. "What do you want?"

"I think he wants what's in your pockets," Sam said.

Damont grinned and pulled his pockets inside out. "Nothing." A few popcorn crumbs fell to the ground. "Shows how smart *he* is."

Sam and Joe exchanged looks.

"You used *popcorn* to leave a trail for yourself through the maze." Joe said.

"Oh!" Wishbone looked up at Damont. "That's why the popcorn led right to the exit door."

"Yeah," Sam said. "That way, you could get through the maze faster."

Damont frowned. "So what?" He eyed the coupon in Joe's hand. "I guess you drew the big prize. I don't need to hang around here." He turned and walked off.

Joe bent over and snapped Wishbone's leash onto his collar. "I'll bet you knew the popcorn was left by Damont, didn't you, boy? Good job!"

"I did? . . . Oh, I did!" Wishbone wagged his tail. "Is that good for a treat?"

Sam leaned toward Joe and looked at his coupon. "I can hardly wait to see how the game works."

"Me, too." Joe and David spoke at the same time. They grinned.

"Come on," Joe said. "Let's go to the prize booth."

The three kids ran off. Wishbone trailed behind Joe.

Reaching the booth, Joe sniffed the air. "We must be close to the popcorn machine. That smell is making me hungry."

"Get some—get some—get some!" Wishbone jumped around at Joe's feet.

David and Sam felt the same way.

Joe showed his coupon to the lady at a booth.

She smiled. "Oh, my goodness, you're the big winner! Congratulations!"

"Thanks," Joe said.

Through a loudspeaker, the woman announced to everyone at the carnival that Joe had won the computer game.

David stepped up to get his pack of gum. Some other kids came by and gave Joe high-fives.

"Joe, you're famous!" Wishbone wagged his tail. All of a sudden, the puppy spotted Ellen and Wanda. "Over here!" He barked and jumped excitedly.

Ellen and Wanda waved, then hurried over.

Joe held up Space Jumpers. "Mom, Miss Gilmore, I won the big prize!"

"That's great, Joe." Ellen smiled.

"And Ellen, you won't believe what else happened to us," Wishbone said.

"Do you want to come back to my house?" Joe asked Sam and David. "We can make popcorn and try out the game."

"Helllooo! The puppy was talking." Wishbone snapped his head in Joe's direction. "Did you say *popcorn?*"

"Maybe you'll let me have a try at that thing." Wanda pointed to the game.

"Sure, Miss Gilmore," Joe said, as everyone walked toward the parking lot.

Wishbone raced ahead, pulling Joe. Sam and David were right behind. "First one who gets to the car wins his own bowl of popcorn," he called out. Wishbone stopped at Ellen's car and wagged his tail. "Oh, look. That would be me!"

About "Hansel and Gretel"

"Hansel and Gretel" is one of the most famous short stories that Jakob and Wilhelm Grimm collected. The story was told only aloud until the Grimm brothers decided to write it down. They did that because they were afraid the story would change if they didn't record its exact wording. They wanted to save "Hansel and Gretel" for the future just the way it was. They wrote it down as close as they could to the way it had been told for so long.

Jakob and Wilhelm Grimm tried not to change any of the oral stories they collected and wrote down. Their first published book of collected folktales was called *Household Tales*. It was published in two separate editions. The first volume came out in 1812. It had eighty-six stories. The second volume came out in 1815. It had seventy tales. In 1857, fifty-four more stories were added, bringing the total to two hundred ten tales. Today we call the complete collection of stories *Grimm's Fairy Tales*.

About Vivian Sathre

Vivian Sathre grew up as the youngest of seven children. She didn't always like being the youngest, or the smallest. But it did have its good points—there was almost always someone around to read to her!

Very few houses were in the neighborhood in which Vivian grew up. Often, there were very few kids to play with. So Vivian spent a lot of time reading. She remembers dropping a bread-crumb trail in an empty lot behind her house after hearing the story "Hansel and Gretel." She wasn't getting ready to leave home, though. And she could see her house all the while she was dropping the crumbs. She just wanted to see if the birds would come and eat them. They never did, at least not when she was around.

Vivian has written many books for young readers. She loves writing for children—it allows her to pretend she's a child again. Depending on how young she wishes to feel, she writes picture books, chapter books, or books for middle-grade readers.

Today, Vivian is a full-time writer and feels lucky to have a career she loves. She really enjoys writing for WISHBONE. But writing means spending a lot of time at her computer. So she always looks forward to her school visits. Talking with kids is a real treat for her!

Vivian lives near Seattle, Washington, with her husband, Roger. They have three grown children: Erika, Mitchell, and Karsten. Vivian had a number of dogs while she was growing up. Right now she has two house cats, but no dogs. But, please! Don't tell Wishbone!